Whatamelon Baby!!!

*The period my poems disappear considers
everything is done.*

Whatamelon Baby

*The period my poems disappear considers
everything is done.*

REX JOVAKIM JOSEPH

First published by
Papertowns Publishers
72, Vishwanath Dham Colony,
Niwaru Road, Jhotwara,
Jaipur, 302012

Whatamelon Baby
Copyright ©Rex Jovakim Joseph, 2023

ISBN Print Book –978-93-94670-95-2

Although the author and publisher have made every effort to ensure the accuracy and completeness of information contained in this book, we assume no responsibility for errors, inaccuracies, omissions, or any inconsistencies herein. Any slights on people, places, or organizations are unintentional.

Printed in India

Cover Design by Ishita Agarwal
Instagram ID- @spotlight_graphics_
@Ishitaagarwal9022@gmail.com

The characters in this book are purely fictional.

The characters involved don't exist in this universe.

They may exist in a parallel universe.

I know my writings are super shit and weird; I fail to follow the basic rules of English Literature, but still, I try to entertain my readers and try my level best to take them for a literature ride through my thoughts and characters. Thank you so much for accepting my work, and I will be sedulous to bring quality content.

Contents

About The Author

Rex Jovakim Joseph is a Software engineer, an entrepreneur with insight, an Investor for a reason, and in addition to all this, a student who is striving to add up his title as a lawyer - *LLB in Criminology at Middlesex University Dubai, MBA at Lincoln University Malaysia, MSW at Sangai University and MA in political science at Lovely Professional University Punjab.* During the first year of undergraduate studies, the lad climbed the wall of entrepreneurship and added the tag of CEO to his name. The journey was never easy, but no tides were big enough to end his passions and dreams. He has published two books - *"It's too big to grab", and "Basorexia of a naughty dirty brat".*

Dedication

For the people who inspired me to write and think.

Foreword

It's not easy to give wings to your dreams, but those who dare to do it are unstoppable. My friend *Rex Jovakim Joseph* has not only given wings to his writing career, he has also reached a lot above the sky to a place that avows your good deeds. My friendship with Rex started on a very strange note, but the more I got to know him, the more I knew this person is very witty, outspoken, understanding, and has uncountable inbuilt talent. I read his books and was mesmerised by his way of putting emotions into words. I believe his writing has a spark that can ignite anyone's hidden emotions.

When I read *"Whatamelon Baby!!!"*, I knew I would be speechless. Conveying emotions that are so appropriate, writing that is so structured, and meanings that are so heart-touching are not in everyone's capabilities. Experiencing emotional chaos and putting it in words are totally divergent scenarios, and my friend has always made that possible so that his book connects directly with the reader's thoughts.

The moments described in this book will bring solace to those who are not at peace and a sense of belonging to those who are somewhere lost.

I Wish my friend lots of success in his writing career.

Happy Reading!

Adv.Megha Bhatia

Moment 1
Briskly Walk On A Sultry Day

When I went for a walk on a sultry day,

There was a whiff of approaching spring.

The faint stuffy smell of hot tar highway;

alerted my brain to grab a sip from the can,

indicating that I was worn out to reach the

destination.

In my view, it was a remote, lonely deserted desert;

I was confused about continuing my steps.

However, the sensual, luscious cactus plant

invited me for a soothing touch.

The moment I felt the communication;

of the needle headed pins of the abandoned

creature,

my nerve was activated, signalling me not to get

attached.

Moment 2
Rapture Wish

It was just a customary sunny hour,
and I let my thoughts get dry.
A sudden drizzle of water drops soaked my heart,
and I let my feelings get wet.
Situations co-occurred, which dumped me to hell,
and I sought for 11:11 to happen to fulfil a desire.
Then I realised that I loathed odd numbers.

Moment 3
Idyllic Routine

When I was about to be in ecstasiate,

you gifted me a bunch of snogs

and erased my usual matutolypea.

When I overthink an elvagyodas,

You presented me with thousands of mirabilia

and asked me not to absquatulate.

My final coruscate helped me become an Elysian.

Everything was just a kopfkino which

I repeat as a routine, like a nefilibata.

Moment 4
Sleeky Ode Curved By A Rough Nib

Your swamp was unwonted, making me rapturous,

leading to a complete pauper in the life of eternity.

It wasn't a lecherous fervent to make you mine;

instead, try to be a philocalist.

I was so smitten by you that

I pleaded to the sun not to be brighter than you.

Booboo, you will be my memoir that was decided

years ago.

Will remain in quietude till you enamour me.

My rectitude for existence will be written as an

appendage

wurkus to write our favourite ode.

Moments 5
Meliorate

Everything she believed was her friend's furphy
tales,
which appeared to be a jayus in type to digest
completely.
Though I was a paralian, I never desired to be an
orarian.
Still, I sang an aubade to soothe her unpleasant
thoughts
and to eradicate the cloud of isolation to create
gaiety.
Compliment my talks with your lengthy
mellifluous lyrics;
Zuiveren, with your presence, let me be a
luftmensch;
Moxie, my acts and pushing my character to be a
thalassophile;
Period I lost my morgenfrisk, and I untagged
myself as a logastellus,
because I was moonstruck by your absence.

Moment 6
Inaugural Love

Made balter moves with the ocean waves and
quivered the craft;
Whenever it kissed the shores and branches,
it wasn't a ruhe act,
A complete chrysalism when the formation was set
free by the hills;
The pines were scabulous whenever she pierced
those lazy branches.
Her slight abate in force is one of the reasons
behind the peiskos;
And those warm curves construct a bridge of xeno
with the mates, to take them for a boketo to a
strange island of lost affections;
Where men have been in vernorexia and lost their
lives for unknown reasons.
Accord men to be with the curves and in
gezelligeid, Authentic them to explore oleka so
that they could, save themselves from being
isolated and transilient from existence.

Moment 7
Luminous Cafe

The day we found that we were noceur,

to the day our hearts were at ease.

The ecstatic shock transferred at the cafe

still lights me up to feed on your existence.

It's you who asked me to do shoshin together;

It's you who forced me to be a stargazer.

My feyre leannan, I will freeze you in summer and heat

you in winter;

With the wabisabi within me that was created by your

presence.

These acts are performed because

I don't want to be in a state of la douleur exquise.

Let's experience aspaldiko when the cloudbursts in

Sahara,

so that we could visit the benthic

and build a castle to witness the mangata

on Atlantis to make wishes together.

Let angels see our welkin and bless us with a baby doll,

so that we could abundantly buss her with agape love.

Everything was a dream of an indolent scriptuerient

writer,

who was in a state as a vemodalen in a ward of

weirdness.

Moment 8
Essay In Trauma

From the day we met to the day we left, it was easy.
Then started the real trauma between mind and
action.

Moment 9
Endangered Human

You made me an opacarophile,
and your sudden departure made me realise that I
am in a tuqburni.
Hey stranger, you are the necessary covetousness,
and I will be craving it.
I believe in stupid retrouvaille that you will be
bidding farewell one day.

Moment 10
Naked Dreams

Nothing better than holding your mitt and my

steering disc.

Nothing better than pecking your forehead and

chanting rhymes.

I scream all night and kick my stress with the

frames on the wall.

Lean back and enjoy my distress.

Moment 11
I Was Locked In Armenia

On the busy alleys of West-Asian landlocked
limits,
I locked her pinkie as we walked through the
burgh.

Together we listened to the monophonic rhythms
of rabiz,
and gifted the chanters drams to play for the
crowd.

I unveiled her golden fleece amid an arrayed group,
to capture portraits of my charm with the canon
lens box.

Moistened our dried lips with the sweet ooze that
led to an unstoppable act of passionate lock.

When our taste buds were frozen, battered pastries
were chosen from the vast that buttered the
cravings.

Then, as the lights began to dim, we rushed into
the pod;
Enjoyed a carnal play, allowing her to laze on my
hub.

Ting! Tong! Ting! Tong!
The note from the log prompts me of her egress.
The taste for tones, craft, literature, and craziness;
never be succeeded because it's created for the
shadow.
Frozen body in need of a warm scarlet rush,
I desire your hard touch, that can activate me.

Moment 12
Lad Comeback Soon

Optics validated that you
are the precious jewels I quest
the jiff I saw you in the lounge.
The craziest soul who struck my heart.
Please live or die on my shoulders
Can't run away from the presence of yours

See haven on your shining orbs,
and fascinated completely.
Every hour reminds your twinkle.
For the cause, hearts are liable.
The day I pause to think of you,
is the day I bid farewell to this green.

I wet you with my bitter tears,
cleanse you with my hourly worship;
to fill up the broken core with
the same old crazy excitement,
that parted flatly with the brat
who wishes for the return to survive

Moment 13
Your Majesty

When the sun burns you, I command Zeus to shower you
with drops.
When the rain soaks you, I command Helios to warm
you with rays.
When the snow freezes you, I command Ullr to melt it
down.
Mornings I assign Aether to wake you up from the
queenly base.
Poseidon will shield the craft from the waves on our gala
to Atlantis.
Nefertum, boon me the Arabian scent to lure you on
lustful nights.
Eros conceded with eternal relish to share when you
sob.
Kratos will strengthen you when you fight with your
emotions.
Hypnos will intone a lullaby when you slip me on an egg
moon.
Nyx will cease the cadence when you need my racy care.
Not just the courtesy, but the duty of heaven to the
reigning king and queen of the universe to lodge gaily.

Moment 14
Sail With Me

Do you miss my presence?
Do you miss our talks?
Do you miss our pecks?
Do you miss my nonsense?

Every night, I follow your social feeds
Every night, I write odes for you.
Every night, I draw portraits of you.
Every night, I gather your unique leads.

Everything started with a boastful profile,
And ended as an unknown stranger.
Everything puzzled by your seductive smile,
And it was figured by your anger.

Moment 15
My Lost Sleep

Lights off

Blade rotating

Room degrees decreases

Under the light woolen, blanket asking Almighty

God for a deep sleep

Cotton pillows on two sides to accompany.

Eyes closed

Mind is stable

eerie sound rushes with no sign of visible light in

Waiting for the unconscious state to come

Slowly fell into the darkness in peace and joy.

Moment 16
Baby I Can't Let You Go Away

I won't let anyone gawk at your eyes because,

those orbs are meant to reign my ardour.

I won't let anyone relish your lips because,

those rose tulips are meant to swill my pain.

I won't let anyone rely on your shoulders because,

those bolsters are intended to absorb my tears.

I won't let anyone bruise your bosoms because,

those jubblies are meant to feed my thirst.

Moment 17
Animated Queen

You are my queen, and I am your reigning king
who builds an
empire of poems and weird blethers.
You are my inked canvas, and I am your artist who
draws
scenes with words on your pointed edges.
You are my only solace of comfort, and I am your
constant
midnight raconteur who weaves stories with joy.

You are my distracted library, and I am your
assigned lazy
librarian who collects your genres of pain.
You are my shuffled playlist, and I am your
composer
who creates albums to cheer you up at our get-
together.

Moment 18
Beatific Moon

Hey skinny ludic soul, How have you been in a
boundary?
Get out of the latibule of fear and enjoy the kensho in
you.
Can we be tristful on our brew date in the presence of a
suton?
So that we could be solasta together in a never-ending
stream.
Sponge ourselves in exhydria and rest on my perfect
vein.

I will take you to an aesthetic atelier on a tindah evening
and ask the artiste to turn you into an angel of aligerous;
in an Annasach tradition to explore each other silently.

I need to apricate you and cast out the purest form of
yours,
with no more dolent series of happenings by toppling
the title of an autophile,
because now you are shadowed by my pure spirits.

Moment 19
You Are Not Anymore

Can you cuddle me deeply for hours?
Visit our nearby chapel in your,
Dad's sedan to plea for our extant;
Together in doting forever.

Can you repose on my bruised bosoms?
Binding me in your protective arms;
And promise that I won't be alone,
Under any position again.

Can you stop digging into my past?
It's you who take matters further and,
Concluded that I was known to you,
On the first day, we met at the cafe.

Oh Lord, grant me a memory loss;
Because every single vocable,
Rhyme like a chant periodically,
Which dumps me into a frozen hell.

Xyz Talk 1

Z: I was once congenial with him.

Y: what happened then?

Z: He's no more solace to me

Xyz Talk 2

X: I'm in love with Alaknanda.

Y: Who is she?

X: a baby idiot who does a cameo in my
manifestation.

Xyz Talk *3*

Z: What's your favorite song?

X: Anything reminds me of comeback.

Z: Can you sing it forever? Until it's detached.

Xyz Talk 4

X: how much should I pay you to stay?

1000$!

Z: something more valuable.

X: go for it.

Z: unlimited snogs followed by a promise.

Acknowledgement

To my father and mother, for your love and care.

To my sister, Ann Mary, for tolerating my weird shits.

To my Poikayil family members for the love and prayers.

To my uncle Johnson Francis, for being my support.

To my brother, Malcolm Anto, for countless assistance.

To my Neethu Miss and CSE B Family for your constant support.

To all my MDX Dubai friends and faculties.

To my dubai mates who keep on insisting me to do weird shits.

To all my haters, for giving me a podium to perform well.

Thanks to my ABBA Father for this life on earth.

Author's Best Selling Books

1. *Basorexia Of A Naughty Dirty Brat*

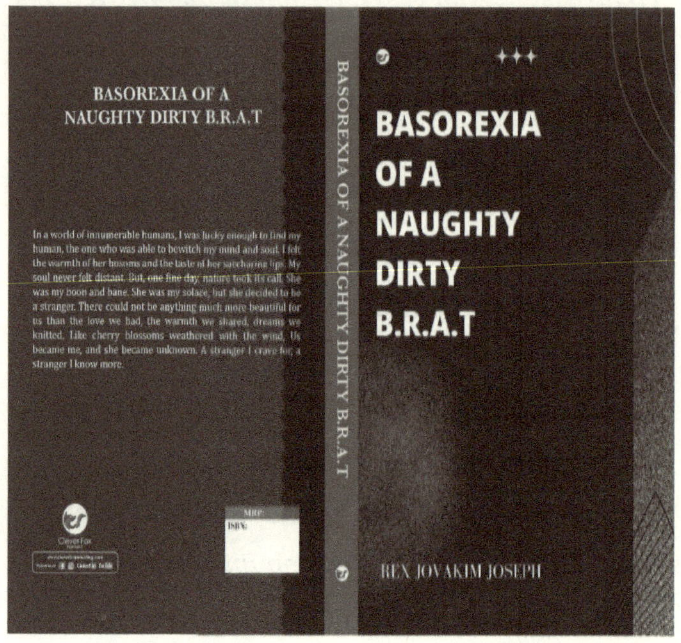

4/5 · Goodreads   4.5/5 · Amazon

- LIFT AWARDS BEST BOOK (POETRY)
- TAGORE SAHITYA SAMMAN - THE LITERARY AWARD 2022

4.5/5 · Goodreads   4.5/5 ·Amazon

- BEST FICTION BOOK 2002 BY THE INDIAN AWAZ FOUNDATION

- TOP 10 FICTION BOOKS OF THE MONTH BY THE DELHI WIRE

SARA
FROM
SYRIA
REX JOVAKIM JOSEPH